BEAR ABOUT TOWN

Written by Stella Blackstone
Illustrated by Debbie Harter

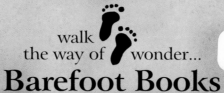

walk
the way of wonder...
Barefoot Books

Bear goes to town every day.

He likes to
walk all the way.

On Monday,
he goes to the bakery.

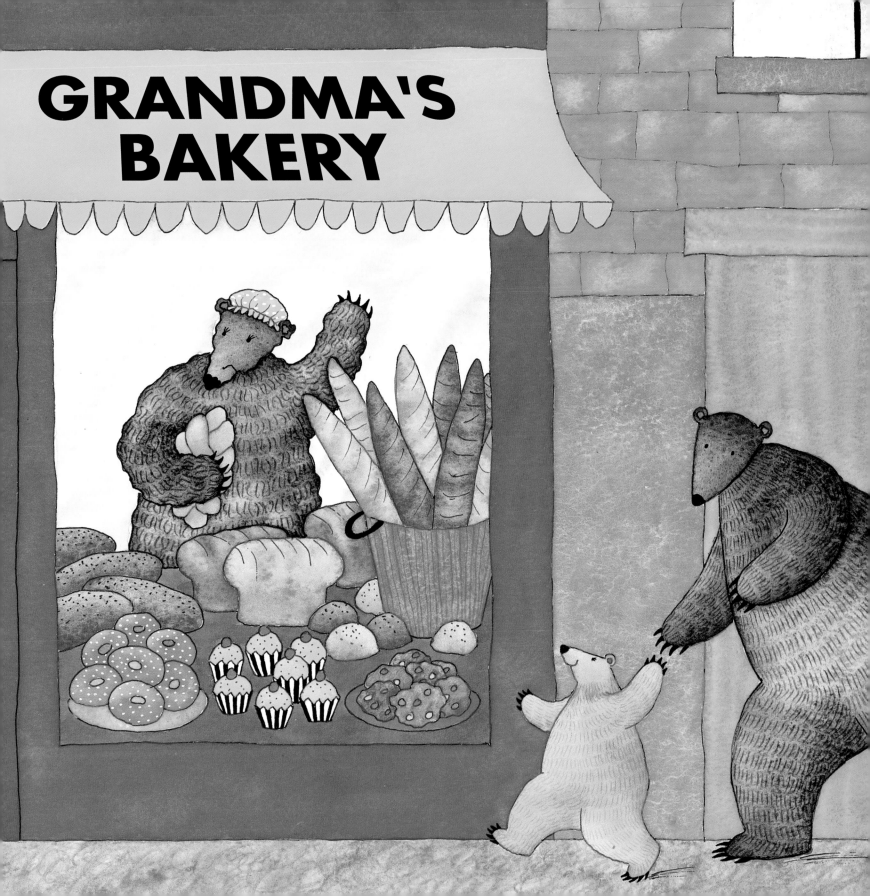

On Tuesday,
he goes for a swim.

On Wednesday,
he watches a movie.

On Thursday,
he visits the gym.

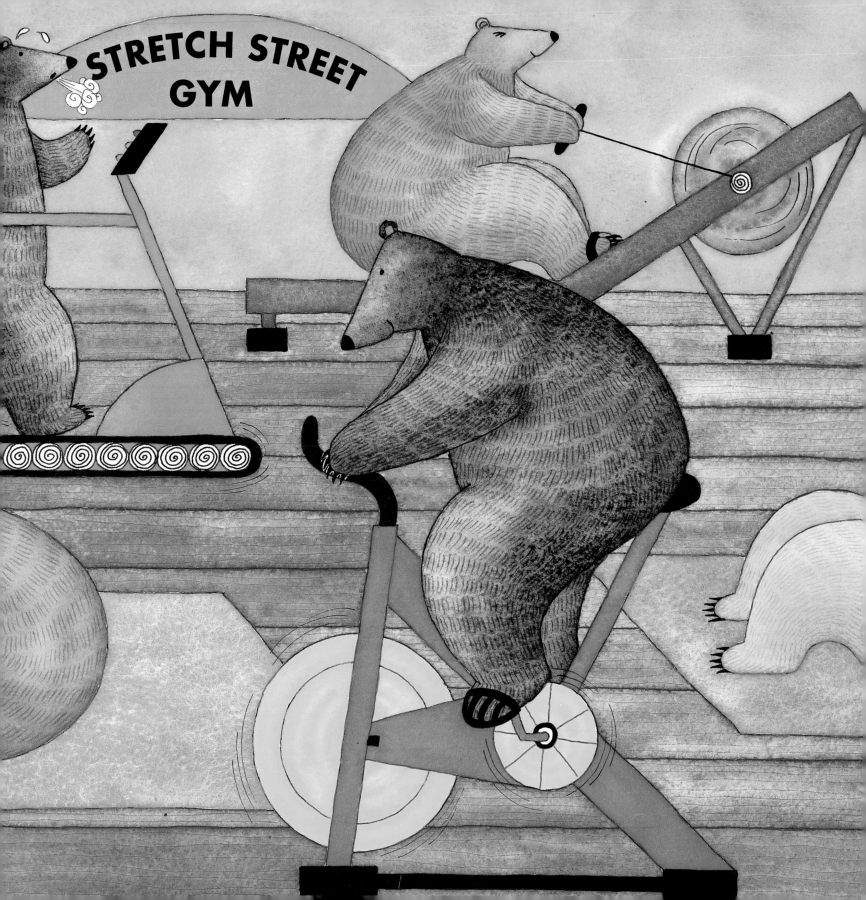

**On Friday,
he goes to the toystore.**

On Saturday, he strolls through the park.

And plays with his friends until dark.

To Annabel and Dominic – S.B.
To Rosemary, John, Evelyn, Richard,
Rosie and Mary – D.H.

Barefoot Books
37 West 17th Street
4th Floor East
New York, New York 10011

Text copyright © 2000 by Stella Blackstone
Illustrations copyright © 2000 by Debbie Harter
The moral right of Stella Blackstone to be identified as the author
and Debbie Harter to be identified as the illustrator
of this work has been asserted

This book was typeset in Futura. The illustrations were prepared in
watercolor, pen and ink and crayon on thick watercolor paper

Graphic design by Tom Grzelinski, England
Color separation by Grafiscan, Italy
Printed and bound in Singapore by Tien Wah Press (Pte) Ltd

This book has been printed on 100% acid-free paper

1 3 5 7 9 8 6 4 2

Cataloging data prepared for the hardback edition (2000)

U.S. Cataloging-in-Publication Data (Library of Congress Standards)

Blackstone, Stella.
    Bear about town / written by Stella Blackstone ;
illustrated by Debbie Harter.—1st ed.
[24]p. : col. ill. ; cm.
Summary: The big, friendly bear goes on his daily walk through his
neighborhood meeting the people who live and work nearby.
ISBN 1-902283-57-0   ISBN 1-84148-152-1 (pbk.)
1. Neighborhood — Fiction. 2. Bears —Fiction. I. Harter, Debbie, ill.
II. Title.
    [E]--dc21 2000   AC   CIP